WILL YOU SURVIVE?

Paul Beck

becker&mayer! kids

CONTENTS

CHOOSE YOUR PATH TO SURVIVAL

The world is full of venomous creatures, fierce animals, hazards, accidents, disasters, and just plain unpleasant situations. It's not everyone who goes looking for such things, but maybe you're just the sort of adventurer who seeks them out.

In this book you'll take a journey through danger and adventure, but you won't just be following along. At every turn you'll have a choice to make, and the actions you choose will determine your path through the rest of the trip.

Do you have what it takes to return from your journey unscathed? In other words, will you survive? Turn the page and find out!

 You should **NEVER** put yourself in dangerous situations to test whether the advice in this book really works. The publisher cannot accept responsibility for any injuries, damage, loss, or prosecutions resulting from the information in this book.

YOUR ADVENTURE BEGINS

BORNEO

ONE SUMMER, you decide it's time for an adventure. You travel to the island of Borneo, where you spend a week swimming in the ocean, hiking in the rain forest, and basking in the tropical weather. As the end of the week gets close, you're really not looking forward to going back, so you put off packing till the last minute. All of a sudden it's the morning of your flight. You rush around, nearly forgetting your plane ticket, and run out of your rented cabin in a panic. You startle a snake, which lunges at your ankle. YOU'VE BEEN BITTEN! What do you do?

CHOOSE YOUR SURVIVAL

OPTION 1

Suck the venom out of the wound.

(JUMP TO PAGE 6.)

OPTION 2

Seek immediate medical attention.

(JUMP TO PAGE 8.)

OPTION 3

Proceed to the airport, uncertain if the snake was poisonous.

(JUMP TO PAGE 10.)

VENOMOUS
SNAKE BITE

OPTION 1
Suck the venom
out of the wound.

NOT THE BEST CHOICE

Trying to suck the venom out of a snakebite
can actually make things worse.

Remembering a cowboy movie where the hero saved himself
from a rattlesnake bite, you make a couple of X-shaped
cuts with your pocketknife (ouch!) where the snake's fangs
went in. Your daily stretching routine has made you just
flexible enough to suck some blood and (you hope!) venom
out of the wound. As you spit the blood out on the ground,
you wonder if this was the best thing to do.

Doctors say this traditional snakebite treatment does
nothing to help—and can even make things worse. You won't
get much venom out. Cutting and sucking on the wound can
damage blood vessels and nerves. Worse, your mouth is now
chock full of bacteria that could lead to an infection,
even if you survive the snakebite.

SNAKE BITE SUCKER

The sort-of good news is that there's still time to get help if you can get to a hospital within a couple of hours. That is, unless the snake that bit you was a cobra. If it was, you'll need antivenom right away, or you're done for.

THERE'S BARELY STILL TIME TO GET HELP!

JUMP BACK TO **PAGE 5** & CHOOSE A BETTER OPTION

VENOMOUS
SNAKE BITE

OPTION 2

Seek medical
attention.

GOOD CHOICE!

Immediate medical attention
is the key to surviving
a venomous snakebite.

YOUR ADVENTURE CONTINUES
HIMALAYAN PLANE CRASH

Your cab driver rushes you to the nearest hospital, where lab tests and your description of the snake confirm that you've been bitten by a pit viper! Emergency room professionals inject you with antivenom and keep you under observation to make sure it takes effect. After 24 hours you're cleared for travel.

You catch the next flight out of the airport. Exhausted from your ordeal, you fall asleep before takeoff and miss the announcement of the plane's destination. Unknown to you, you're on the wrong flight! Worse, sometime later you're startled awake by loud alarms in the cabin. Out the window you see snowy peaks rushing up at you. You're about to crash-land in the Himalayas!

You survive the crash, but you're hungry, still weak from snakebite, dressed for tropical weather, and have no idea where you are. What do you do?

CHOOSE YOUR SURVIVAL

OPTION 1

Attempt to climb down the mountain.

(JUMP TO PAGE 12.)

OPTION 2

Take shelter in a nearby cave.

(JUMP TO PAGE 14.)

OPTION 3

Stay in the plane and hope someone will find you.

(JUMP TO PAGE 16.)

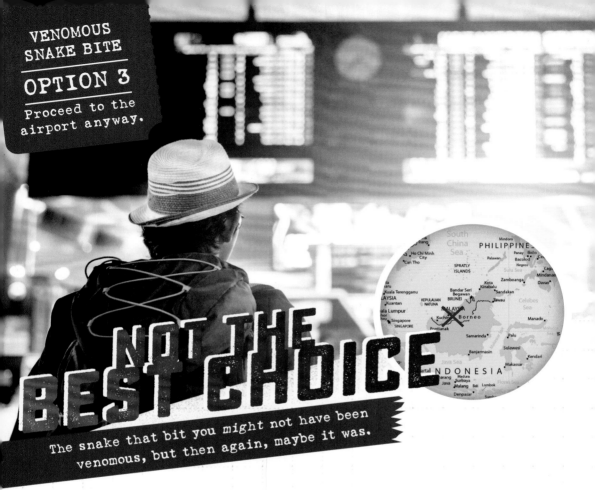

NOT THE BEST CHOICE

The snake that bit you might not have been
venomous, but then again, maybe it was.

You didn't get a good look at the snake before it
slithered away, but you remember from your travel guide
that most of the venomous snakes in Borneo are sea snakes.
Since you're on land, you figure it's more than likely the
snake you startled wasn't venomous. Ignoring the small
voice inside you that wonders why a non-venomous snake
would have bitten you in the first place, you rush to the
airport just in time to catch your plane.

You get on board. The pain in your ankle isn't getting any better. As you make your way down the aisle to your seat, you begin to feel sick to your stomach. Your arms feel weak as you struggle to lift your backpack into the overhead compartment. When you finally drop into your seat, you realize these are exactly the venomous snakebite symptoms you've read about.

You're in luck! Or at least lucky for someone who started their trip by being bitten by a venomous snake. The crew hasn't yet closed the doors to the plane.

GET OFF THE PLANE RIGHT AWAY!

JUMP BACK TO **PAGE 5** & CHOOSE A BETTER OPTION

NOT THE BEST CHOICE

You're not dressed for a trek in the
mountains, and besides, you have no idea
which direction help is in.

You grab the pack of pretzels you had put in the seat pocket in
front of you, stuff them in your pocket, and climb quickly out
of the emergency exit. You take a look at your surroundings. The
plane has come down on a wide ridge. A high mountain peak rises
above, covered with snow. On one side of the ridge a boulder-
covered slope drops steeply into a valley with a stream at the
bottom. If you went that way, at least there would be water. On
the other side there's a cliff, but you could probably find a
way down. Or you could hike down along the ridge. The problem
(or one of them!) is that you have no idea which way (if any!)
leads to help. You don't see any paths, buildings, or people.
The sun will go down soon, and you're already feeling chilly.

Besides, it's certain that air traffic control knows your plane has gone down. Rescue crews will be searching for it. It could be your imagination, but you think you might even hear the faint sound of a helicopter. Wouldn't it be a better idea to stay nearby?

IT'S PROBABLY BEST TO STAY NEAR THE CRASH SITE

JUMP BACK TO PAGE 9 & CHOOSE A BETTER OPTION

HIMILAYAN
PLANE CRASH

OPTION 2
Take shelter in
a nearby cave

GOOD CHOICE!

The cave will provide better
shelter than the wrecked
plane.

YOUR ADVENTURE CONTINUES
SNOW LEOPARD ENCOUNTER

You take the airplane blanket and the small pillow you had at
your seat and head into the cave. The floor is dry, and there
might even be a flat spot to lie down in later. You think you
should probably stay close to the entrance so you can keep an
eye out for rescuers. But you decide to go a little farther in,
just to get out of the wind. It's dark toward the back, and you
can't tell how far it goes.

Suddenly you hear a low growl. You're not alone in the cave!
There's a snow leopard crouched in the shadows. It lowers its
head, and its long tail gives a twitch. What do you do?

CHOOSE YOUR SURVIVAL

OPTION 1
Run away.

(JUMP TO PAGE 18.)

OPTION 2
Attack the leopard before it attacks you.

(JUMP TO PAGE 20.)

OPTION 3
Back away slowly out of the cave.

(JUMP TO PAGE 22.)

HIMALAYAN
PLANE CRASH

OPTION 3

Stay in the plane
& hope rescuers
will find you.

NOT THE BEST CHOICE

The most important thing to do after
a plane crash is get out of the plane.

Your plane just came down on its belly on the side of a
mountain! Amazingly enough, you're not injured. You're not
even sore, except for your ankle where the snake bit you.
The plane, on the other hand, isn't in such great shape.
At least it's in a more or less level spot. Out the window
you can see the wing and a crumpled engine. You can't tell
for sure, but you think there might be smoke coming out
of the engine. You smell jet fuel. You need shelter in
the high mountains, but the biggest danger now is fire.
It's not just danger from flames. If the cabin fills with
smoke, you won't survive if you don't get out fast.

Based on the number of travelers and the number of miles traveled, plane accidents are very, very (very!) rare. Of course, it probably doesn't make you feel any better to know that the crash-landing you just experienced doesn't happen very often. Still, among those people unlucky enough to be in aircraft accidents, more than 95% survive.

INSIDE A JUST-CRASHED PLANE ISN'T A GOOD PLACE TO STAY

JUMP BACK TO **PAGE 9**
& CHOOSE A BETTER OPTION

NOT THE BEST CHOICE

Big cats hunt by stalking and then chasing down their prey.

Can you run faster than a snow leopard? You remember seeing a TV show where one of them chased a wild goat down the side of a mountain. You don't remember whether the leopard caught its prey, but you know you're not as fast or sure-footed as a goat. On the other hand, you remember reading that snow leopards aren't aggressive toward humans and aren't known to attack them. On the other hand (do you have a third hand?), you're between this one and the exit, and its claws and teeth look really sharp.

Snow leopards may not be known to attack humans, but there's a lot that people don't know about these elusive hunters. In any case, running is never a good way to escape from a big cat. They make their living catching animals that run faster than people can. Also, running down the side of a rocky, snowy mountain isn't a good idea even if there's nothing chasing you. You could twist an ankle or seriously hurt yourself in a fall.

SNOW LEOPARDS MAY NOT ATTACK HUMANS, BUT RUNNING ISN'T THE BEST OPTION

JUMP BACK TO **PAGE 15** & CHOOSE A BETTER OPTION

SNOW LEOPARD
ENCOUNTER

OPTION 2

Attack the
leopard before it
attacks you.

NOT THE BEST CHOICE

The leopard will fight back, and it has
better weapons than you do.

Snow leopards can grow to be more than 4 feet long (1.2 m), not counting the tail. That's almost as long as the rest of the leopard's body, and the longest tail of any cat. Snow leopards can weigh as much as 120 pounds (54 kg). Their huge paws are built for sure-footed running on snow and rocks, and their powerful legs can carry them as far as 25 feet (7.6 m) in a single leap. Snow leopards hunt wild sheep and goats, along with smaller mountain animals like marmots and birds. Stealthy and camouflaged, the leopard stalks its prey until it gets within about 30 feet (9 m), then closes the distance with a sprint and a pounce.

There's a lot scientists still don't know about snow leopards in the wild, but these cats aren't known to attack humans. However, one sure way to make a snow leopard defend itself would be for you to attack it first. A snow leopard can bring down prey as big as three times its own weight. Its strength, claws, and teeth are more than a match for a human.

DON'T PICK AN UNNECESSARY FIGHT THAT YOU CAN'T WIN

JUMP BACK TO **PAGE 15** & CHOOSE A BETTER OPTION

GOOD CHOICE!

Snow leopards prefer to
stay away from people.

YOUR ADVENTURE CONTINUES

BASE CAMP, HIMALAYAS

You back out of the cave. Watching you cautiously, the snow leopard glides out and disappears up the side of the mountain. Its camouflage makes it nearly invisible. You bed down for the night just inside the cave entrance. In the morning you wake to the sound of a helicopter. Rescue has arrived!

The helicopter flies you to a mountaineering base camp, then heads back to get more survivors. Climbers at the base camp have just come down from the summit. They give you spare warm clothes. You're lacing your new shoes when you hear a low rumble. You look up to see a boiling cloud of snow coming down the side of the mountain. An avalanche is rushing toward you! What do you do?

CHOOSE YOUR SURVIVAL

OPTION 1

Try to get out of the way as fast as possible.

(JUMP TO PAGE 24.)

OPTION 2

Try to "swim" on top of the avalanche.

(JUMP TO PAGE 26.)

OPTION 3

Create an air pocket around your face as the avalanche stops.

(JUMP TO PAGE 28.)

AVALANCHE

OPTION 1

Try to get out of
the way as fast
as possible.

GOOD START, BUT YOU'LL NEED TO DO MORE

It's best not to get caught by an avalanche.
Unfortunately . . .

You move quickly toward the side of the avalanche's path.
If you can't avoid the rushing snow, at least you'll be
closer to the edge, where it's shallower and less powerful.
But getting out of the way of an avalanche can be tough!
They can race downhill as fast as 80 miles per hour.

Unfortunately you don't have time to figure out what
kind of avalanche this one is. You're almost out of the
way, but the snow still catches you and knocks you off
your feet!

TYPES OF AVALANCHES

There are two types of avalanches: loose snow and slab. Loose snow avalanches start small and get bigger as they go, gathering more and more snow as they slide down the side of the mountain. They can grow to be large, fast, heavy, and deadly. Slab avalanches are even deadlier. They happen when a huge slab of snow breaks loose from the snow underneath. The whole slab starts moving at once, rushing downhill and breaking up as it goes.

LOOSE SNOW AVALANCHE

SLAB AVALANCHE

YOU'RE CAUGHT IN THE AVALANCHE

JUMP BACK TO **PAGE 23** & CHOOSE A BETTER OPTION

GOOD IDEA, BUT YOU'LL NEED TO DO MORE

Try to stay on top of the snow.

Tibet

HIMALAYA

Nepal

Mount Everest   Bhutan

Kanchenjunga

Bangladesh

India   Myanr

Bay of
Bengal

If you're caught in an avalanche, you need to do everything you can to stay near the top. The closer you are to the surface, the better the chance that rescuers can find you and dig you out.

As the avalanche drags you along, you struggle to stay on the surface. You've heard people call it "swimming," but it's more like thrashing—paddling with your arms, kicking, anything to keep from being buried. As the avalanche begins to slow, you hope you have managed to stay close to the surface.

Almost all of the people who get buried in avalanches are skiers, snowboarders, snowmobilers, or mountaineers who venture across the snow on steep, avalanche-prone slopes. And in almost all of those cases, the avalanche is triggered by the person who gets buried or by someone in their group. It's very rare for an avalanche to sweep down on a victim with no warning from above.

(Un)lucky you! You're caught in a rare avalanche.

YOU'RE BURIED IN THE SNOW

JUMP BACK TO **PAGE 23**
& CHOOSE A BETTER OPTION

AVALANCHE

OPTION 3

Create an air pocket around your face as the avalanche stops.

GOOD CHOICE!

If you get buried by an avalanche, breathing is critical.

YOUR ADVENTURE CONTINUES
DELHI, INDIA

You're tumbling along in the avalanche! As the snow slows, you remember to create an air pocket before you come to a stop, so you can breathe. You also manage to stick an arm upward in the hope that your hand will be visible above the snow. Luckily, rescuers spot you right away and dig you out.

You leave the base camp with the climbers and eventually make your way to Kathmandu. After your last air travel experience, you're not ready to board a plane, so you decide to go by land to Delhi, India. On the way, you stop to visit a wildlife sanctuary. You get out of the tour jeep to take a picture of a rhinoceros. Eyes on your camera, you don't notice that you've wandered far from the jeep. Suddenly the rhino charges! What do you do?

CHOOSE YOUR SURVIVAL

OPTION 1
Run away.

(JUMP TO PAGE 30.)

OPTION 2
Climb a tree.

(JUMP TO PAGE 32.)

OPTION 3
Drop to the ground.

(JUMP TO PAGE 34.)

OPTION 1

Run Away.

The horn is impressive, but the Indian rhino's real weapon of choice is its lower canine teeth. They're long and dangerous.

NOT THE BEST CHOICE

You can't outrun a rhino.

CHINA

NEPAL

New Delhi

Kathmandu

INDIA

The rhinoceros may look big and heavy (and it is!), but that doesn't mean it's clumsy or slow. A charging Indian rhino can run as fast as 30 miles an hour (48 km/h). If you were Usain Bolt (are you?) you might be able to outrun it. If you're not the world's fastest human sprinter, you don't stand a chance. And don't think you could dodge out of the way with fancy footwork. A rhino can turn on a dime.

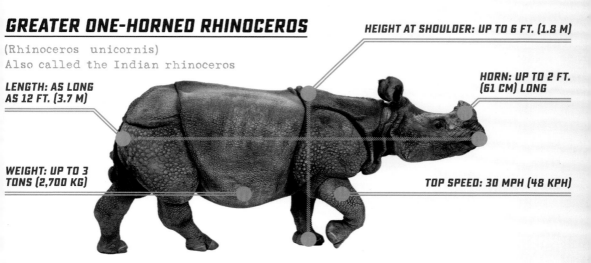

GREATER ONE-HORNED RHINOCEROS

(Rhinoceros unicornis)
Also called the Indian rhinoceros

HEIGHT AT SHOULDER: UP TO 6 FT. (1.8 M)

HORN: UP TO 2 FT. (61 CM) LONG

LENGTH: AS LONG AS 12 FT. (3.7 M)

WEIGHT: UP TO 3 TONS (2,700 KG)

TOP SPEED: 30 MPH (48 KPH)

UNLESS YOU ARE THE FASTEST RUNNER ALIVE, YOU'LL NEVER ESCAPE BY RUNNING

JUMP BACK TO PAGE 29 & CHOOSE A BETTER OPTION

YOUR ADVENTURE CONTINUES

INDIA

There's a tree just a few feet away. You sprint to it and climb up into its branches just as the rhino arrives. You wait there, out of reach of its teeth, until it decides you're not a threat and goes away. You go back to the jeep.

At the entrance to the wildlife sanctuary you hire a taxi to take you the rest of the way to Delhi. There's a road closure on the highway. The driver uses GPS to find a detour. Unfortunately, the GPS system has an outdated map. With his eyes on the screen instead of the road, the driver drives right into a deep reservoir! The car begins to sink. What do you do?

CHOOSE YOUR SURVIVAL

OPTION 1
Open your window right away.

(JUMP TO PAGE 36.)

OPTION 2
Open the door.

(JUMP TO PAGE 38.)

OPTION 3
Stay in the car and wait for help.

(JUMP TO PAGE 40.)

Rhinos charge when startled. Sometimes even at inanimate objects like trees.

NOT THE BEST CHOICE

You might be able to roll away at the last second, or you might get trampled.

If the rhino is nearly on top of you and there's absolutely no other way to get away, dropping to the ground would be better than doing nothing. Otherwise it's not a good strategy. Rhinos have sharp senses of hearing and smell, but their eyesight isn't very good. The rhino could charge on by, but it could just as easily run right over you. And with a weight of as much 6,000 pounds, you definitely don't want a greater one-horned rhinoceros trampling you. (Really, it's best not to be trampled by any species of rhinoceros.)

LYING ON THE GROUND WITH A THREE-TON, NEARSIGHTED RHINO BARRELING DOWN ON YOU ISN'T THE BEST STRATEGY

JUMP BACK TO PAGE 29 & CHOOSE A BETTER OPTION

GOOD CHOICE!

The window is the key to
your escape.

YOUR
ADVENTURE
CONTINUES
AUSTRALIA

If the water outside the car rises past the level of the
windows, the pressure against the glass will keep them from
sliding down. So it's important to get the window open right
away, before the car sinks that far. If you can't get it open
far enough to climb out, you'll have to wait for the water
inside to rise far enough to equalize the pressure so you can
open the door. Also, you have to try not to panic. Good luck!

Luckily you manage to lower your window right away, make
your escape, and swim to shore. After you recover, you decide
to go straight to the airport (with a different driver this
time!) and grab the next flight out of the country. It's
a 12-hour trip to Sydney, Australia. You arrive with no
trouble, but just as you're unpacking in your hotel room the
fire alarm goes off. Worse, you smell smoke! What do you do?

CHOOSE YOUR SURVIVAL

OPTION 1

Open the window and yell "Fire!" to get help.

(JUMP TO PAGE 42.)

OPTION 2

Grab the fire extinguisher and go look for the fire.

(JUMP TO PAGE 44.)

OPTION 3

Keep low and head for the exit.

(JUMP TO PAGE 46.)

EXIT

NOT THE BEST CHOICE

Water pressure will keep the door from opening.

If you manage to open the door immediately after the car hits the water, you could get out that way. But that also lets the water in faster, and the car may sink to the bottom before you can get out. If you don't get the door open right away, the difference between the water pressure outside the car and the air pressure inside will make it impossible to open the door. By the time the water has risen only halfway up the door, it's already pressing on it with a force of more than 500 pounds (227 kg)!

If the car sinks, the only way to get the door open is to wait until the car fills most of the way with water. Then the water pressure inside will balance the pressure outside, and you can push the door open. Of course, you'd have to hold your breath for the last part, and you'd still have to get out and swim to the surface.

Water pressure increases about 1/2 pound (.23 kg) per square inch for every foot of depth. That may not sound like much until you realize that the door of a sedan has an area of more than 2,000 square inches (1.3 km).

0.5 POUND/INCH²	1 FOOT
1 POUND/INCH²	2 FEET
1.5 POUNDS/INCH²	3 FEET
2 POUNDS/INCH²	4 FEET
2.5 POUNDS/INCH²	5 FEET
3 POUNDS/INCH²	6 FEET
3.5 POUNDS/INCH²	7 FEET
4 POUNDS/INCH²	8 FEET
4.5 POUNDS/INCH²	9 FEET
5 POUNDS/INCH²	10 FEET

UNLESS YOU GET THE DOOR OPEN BEFORE THE CAR STARTS TO SINK, IT'S NOT THE QUICKEST WAY OUT.

JUMP BACK TO **PAGE 33** & CHOOSE A BETTER OPTION

NOT THE BEST CHOICE

The car will sink and fill with water.

Are you crazy? The car is filling up with water! It will be over your head long before help arrives. You need to get out as quickly as you can. Soon water pressure against the doors will keep you from opening them. And if the water rises above the windows, the pressure will keep you from opening those too.

EMERGENCY HAMMER

It's hard to break a car window when you're inside the car. The windows are made of strong, tempered glass, so feet or fists won't do the trick. There's no room to get a good swing, and unless there happens to be a brick, hammer, or other hard and heavy object in the passenger compartment, there's no good tool you can use to break the glass. Many motorists carry a small hammer made just for breaking car windows in an emergency. The hammer has a pointy metal tip, which concentrates all the force of the blow into one tiny spot. That's enough to start a crack and shatter the window.

If you're trying to break your way out of a car in an emergency, break a side window, not the windshield. The windshield is much stronger—it's a layer of plastic sandwiched between two layers of glass.

WATER PRESSURE WILL TRAP YOU IN THE CAR

! JUMP BACK TO **PAGE 33** & CHOOSE A BETTER OPTION

NOT THE BEST CHOICE

Help is already on the way, and you need to get out now.

The alarm is going off, right? The fire department is already on its way. Unless you're trapped in the room by flames outside the door, what you need to do is get out of the building fast. Now might be a good time to check that sign on the back of the hotel room door telling you where the exit is.

Feel the door and knob with the back of your hand. Is it hot? Then there are flames outside. Stuff a wet towel along the bottom of the door to keep the smoke from coming in. Now you can open the window and shout for help, but be sure to keep the door closed so you're not letting a draft out to feed the flames in the hallway.

The flames are just one of the dangerous parts of a fire. Burning wood, plastic, and other materials in a building fire produce smoke and poisonous gases that are even more deadly. In fact, more people die in fires from smoke inhalation than from burns.

DON'T STAY IN YOUR ROOM UNLESS YOU HAVE NO OTHER CHOICE

!

JUMP BACK TO **PAGE 37**
& CHOOSE A BETTER OPTION

NOT THE BEST CHOICE

Leave the firefighting to the professionals.

Unless you see the fire and know it's small, don't try to put it out. A fire can grow from a small flame to a big blaze in a matter of seconds. Fire extinguishers aren't made for big or fast-spreading fires. And you certainly shouldn't go looking for the fire to try to put it out. Leave that to the firefighters, who have the skills and training for it. Your task is to get out of the hotel.

FIRE EXTINQUISHER TYPES

Different kinds of fires require different extinguishers. The label will tell you what kind of fire the extinguisher works on.

CLASS A: REGULAR COMBUSTIBLES (BURNABLE MATERIALS) LIKE PAPER AND WOOD

CLASS B: BURNING LIQUIDS LIKE GASOLINE AND OIL

CLASS C: BURNING ELECTRICAL OR ELECTRONIC EQUIPMENT

MANY EXTINGUISHERS WILL WORK ON ALL THREE TYPES. THESE ARE LABELED ABC.

There are two other fire classes. Class D fires are burning metal (yes, some metals can burn!), and Class K fires are cooking oil or grease fires. You probably won't ever see a Class D fire, and most Class K fires happen in places like restaurant kitchens.

DON'T GO LOOKING FOR THE FIRE—GET AWAY FROM IT

JUMP BACK TO PAGE 37 & CHOOSE A BETTER OPTION

HOTEL FIRE

OPTION 3
Keep low and head
for the exit.

GOOD CHOICE!
You need to avoid the
smoke and get out of the
building.

YOUR ADVENTURE CONTINUES
AUSTRALIA

After checking the door to see if it's hot (it's not),
you leave the room. There's smoke in the hallway. You
crouch down as you head for the exit. The smoke and
poisonous gases in a fire collect near the ceiling first,
so it's important to stay low. Crawl if you have to. You
make it out of the hotel. Paramedics treat you for smoke
inhalation as you watch the firefighters battle the blaze.

Later, after getting new clothes, a new toothbrush, and
a new hotel, you head to the beach. You're swimming in the
waves when you feel a strong current pulling you away from
the beach. You're being swept out to sea in a rip current!
What do you do?

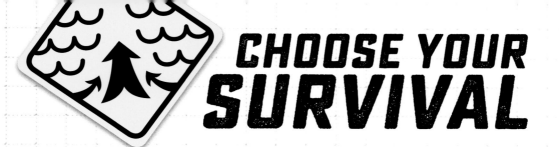

CHOOSE YOUR SURVIVAL

OPTION 1
Swim against the current.

(JUMP TO PAGE 48.)

OPTION 2
Swim parallel to the shore

(JUMP TO PAGE 50.)

OPTION 3
Ride the current out to calmer water.

(JUMP TO PAGE 52.)

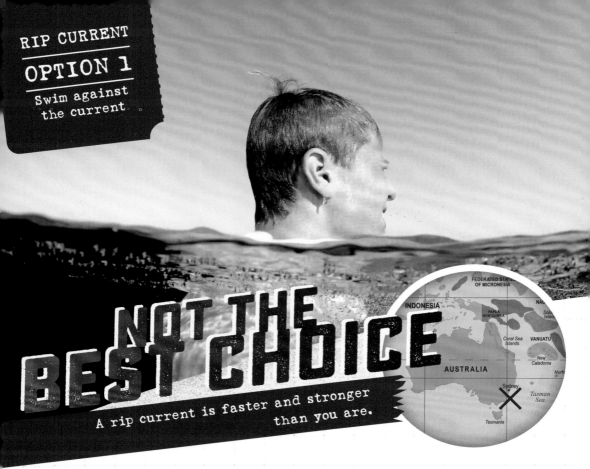

NOT THE BEST CHOICE

A rip current is faster and stronger than you are.

Rip currents form when waves interacting with the shape of the ocean floor or with each other create a fast-moving current headed away from shore. The current may flow at any speed from 1 to as fast as 8 feet per second (.31 to 3.1 kilometers per hour). You can't beat it by swimming. But one good thing (as good as it can be when you're being swept out to sea!) is that a rip current isn't as wide as the whole beach. Of course, it can be anywhere from as wide as a highway to as wide two football fields.

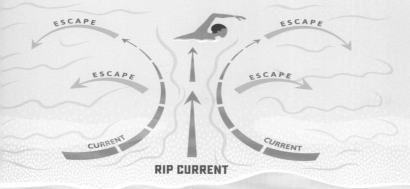

SPOT THE RIP CURRENT

If you pay attention to the waves at the beach, there are clues that can help you spot a rip current.

A GAP IN THE WAVES
If there's a calm-looking area where the waves aren't breaking, it's probably a rip current.

A TRAIL OF FOAM, SAND, AND DEBRIS
Rip currents pull sand and debris away from the shore, often leaving a trail you can see.

YOU CAN'T BEAT THE CURRENT

JUMP BACK TO **PAGE 47**
& CHOOSE A BETTER OPTION

GOOD CHOICE!

Swimming parallel to the
shore is the best way to
escape a rip current.

YOUR ADVENTURE CONTINUES
AUSTRALIA

You swim parallel to the beach instead of trying to fight the current. Eventually you escape the rip current's path and make your way back to shore. It's a tiring trip. You've just reached a spot where your feet can touch the bottom when you feel a sharp pain in your ankle, right where the snake bit you a few days ago. You look down to see a striped fish with a row of long spines on its back. You've been stung by a lionfish! What do you do?

CHOOSE YOUR SURVIVAL

OPTION 1

Perform first aid, then get medical attention.

(JUMP TO PAGE 64.)

OPTION 2

Perform first aid, then apply heat to the wound.

(JUMP TO PAGE 66.)

OPTION 3

Ice the wound.

(JUMP TO PAGE 68.)

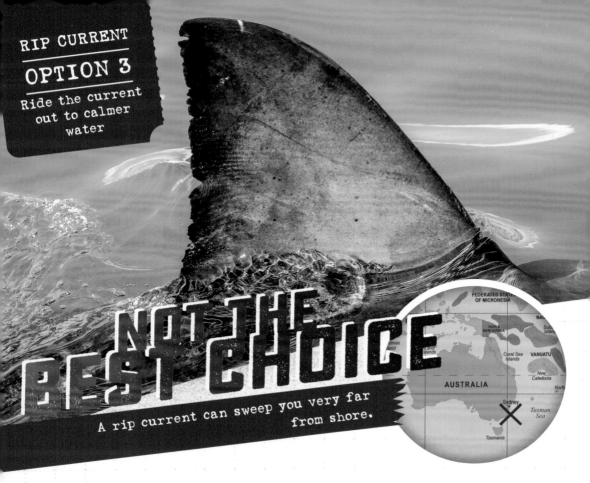

NOT THE BEST CHOICE

A rip current can sweep you very far from shore.

You've heard that rip currents usually break up beyond the surf, so you decide to ride this one out past the breaking waves, then swim back to shore in a different spot. But a large, strong rip current can sweep you hundreds of yards out to sea before it dies out. As you watch the beach get farther and farther away, you think that maybe your decision wasn't the best one. Just when you're wondering how things could get any worse, you see the looming shape of a shark in the water! What do you do?

CHOOSE YOUR SURVIVAL

OPTION 1
Splash and make noise to scare the shark away.

(JUMP TO PAGE 54.)

OPTION 2
Punch the shark in the snout.

(JUMP TO PAGE 56.)

OPTION 3
Stay calm and keep your eyes on the shark.

(JUMP TO PAGE 58.)

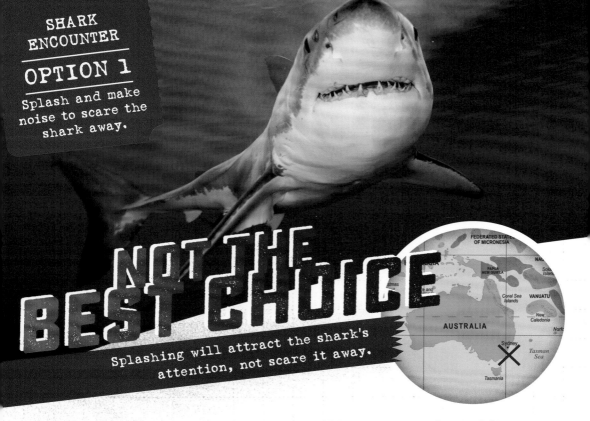

SHARK
ENCOUNTER

OPTION 1
Splash and make
noise to scare the
shark away.

NOT THE BEST CHOICE

Splashing will attract the shark's
attention, not scare it away.

Noisy splashing and thrashing will make you look like an
animal in distress, an easy meal for a cruising shark.
Other things that can attract a shark's attention include
shiny jewelry, which can sparkle like fish scales in
the water, and bright, contrasting colors on swimsuits,
surfboards, or kayaks.

There are hundreds of shark species. Bigger sharks eat
bigger food, so any shark longer than about six feet can be
dangerous to humans. But the top three species responsible
for attacks on humans are the white shark, tiger shark, and
bull shark.

Bull shark (Carcharhinus leucas)

Tiger shark (Galeocerdo cuvier)

White shark (Carcharodon carcharias)

The biggest shark of all is no threat at all. The whale shark (Rhincodon typus) is the size of a school bus but eats only the tiny animals called plankton. It's not only the world's largest shark but the world's largest fish of any kind.

THE LESS YOU LOOK AND ACT LIKE FOOD, THE MORE LIKELY THE SHARK IS TO LEAVE YOU ALONE

WHAT ARE THE CHANCES?

Your chances of being attacked by a shark at the beach are very, very low. Every year, hundreds of millions of people go into the ocean to play, swim, dive, surf, and enjoy the water. But in an average year there are only about 80 unprovoked shark attacks in the whole world, and of those, only six are fatal. You have a better chance of being struck by lightning. (Does that make you feel better about sharks, or worse about lightning?)

JUMP BACK TO **PAGE 53** & CHOOSE A BETTER OPTION

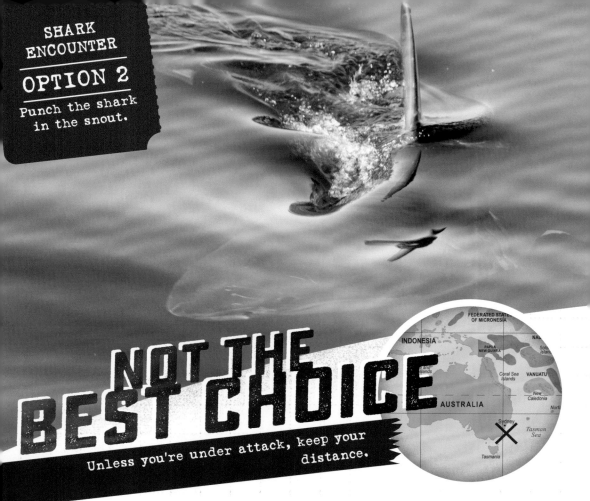

NOT THE BEST CHOICE

Unless you're under attack, keep your distance.

If a shark is attacking you, by all means defend yourself any way you can. A shark's snout is particularly sensitive, so hitting it there can make it keep its distance, at least for a while. The eyes and gills are other vulnerable spots to hit if you need to fight off an attack. But if a shark isn't on the attack, approaching it so you can punch it in the nose it isn't high up on the list of good ideas.

ELECTRO-DETECTOR

A shark's snout and head are covered with thousands of tiny pores called ampullae (am-PULL-ee) of Lorenzini. These are the sensitive detectors for a real sixth sense, the ability to detect electrical activity. A hunting shark can sense the tiny electrical fields created by its prey's nerves and muscles. If your heart is beating extra-fast, it can detect that, too.

Pores

Nerves to brain

Jelly-filled tubes

Sensory cells

▲ Nurse shark

DON'T GIVE THE SHARK A REASON TO SEE YOU AS A THREAT

SHARK ATTACKS

There are three types of unprovoked shark attacks. A hit-and-run attack happens when a shark in the shallow water near the beach mistakes a person for its normal prey. The shark bites, lets go, and leaves. In a sneak attack, a shark attacks its unsuspecting human victim in deeper water, seemingly out of nowhere. In a bump-and-bite attack, the shark circles and hits the victim with its head or body before biting. The two deep-water attacks are the most dangerous.

JUMP BACK TO **PAGE 53** & CHOOSE A BETTER OPTION

SHARK
ENCOUNTER

OPTION 3
Stay calm and
keep your eyes
on the shark.

GOOD CHOICE!
Be wary, but don't give
the shark a reason to be
interested in you.

**DANGER
Quicksand**

YOUR ADVENTURE CONTINUES
AUSTRALIA

You float upright in the water and make yourself seem as large as possible. You keep your movements still and as slow as you can make them while still staying afloat. You keep your eyes on the shark, ready for any sign of attack. It turns toward you, and you do your best to stay calm and keep your heart from beating faster. The shark turns again and swims away.

You start swimming back, but you're very tired. Fortunately, a fisherman comes by in a boat. He takes you aboard and gives you a ride toward the beach. Unfortunately, as you're wading ashore by a stream outlet, you sink up to your knees. It's quicksand! What do you do?

CHOOSE YOUR SURVIVAL

OPTION 1
Pull your legs out quickly.

(JUMP TO PAGE 60.)

OPTION 2
Wiggle your legs to create some space, then pull them out.

(JUMP TO PAGE 62.)

OPTION 3
Swim out of the quicksand on your back.

(JUMP TO PAGE 70.)

NOT THE BEST CHOICE

You won't be able to do it.

Quicksand looks solid, but it's really a mixture of sand and water. If you step in it, you sink down, and your feet and legs push water out of the mixture. That packs the sand tightly around your legs, making it impossible to pull them out. The good news is that, unlike what you may have seen in the movies or on TV, you won't keep sinking until your head disappears beneath the surface. The bad news is that you're stuck. Trying to pull your legs out while standing can cause you to sink deeper and get even more stuck.

Sand is made of tiny grains of rock. In regular sand the grains take up 70 to 75 percent of the volume. But quicksand has very loosely packed grains. As much as 70 percent of the volume is water. If you stand on it, your weight causes the sand to collapse, and you sink down.

TRYING TO PULL YOUR LEGS OUT WHILE STANDING ON THEM WON'T DO THE TRICK

In some desert areas there's a type of quicksand made of sand and air instead of water. You can sink in it, too, but only a couple of inches. After that it's packed too tightly for you to sink more.

JUMP BACK TO **PAGE 59** & CHOOSE A BETTER OPTION

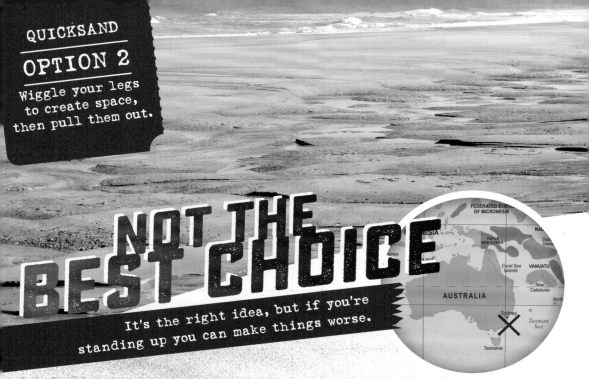

NOT THE BEST CHOICE

It's the right idea, but if you're standing up you can make things worse.

You're stuck in the quicksand because your weight has pushed some of the water out from between the grains of sand. The key to escaping is to get the water back in. Wiggling your legs—slowly!—can help to make space for water to seep back in, but if you're still standing on them you may just work your way deeper into the sand.

Quicksand looks like sand, but in many ways it acts like extra-thick water. It's possible for your body to "float" on it the same way you can float on water. In fact, it's easier, because the quicksand is denser than water. If you can figure out a way to take your weight off your legs, wiggling them might eventually let enough water into the mix to let you pull them out.

GETTING WATER BACK
INTO THE SAND IS THE KEY
BUT YOU NEED TO GET
YOUR WEIGHT OFF
YOUR LEGS

!

JUMP BACK TO **PAGE 59**
& CHOOSE A BETTER OPTION

LIONFISH STING

OPTION 1
Perform first aid, then get medical attention.

GOOD CHOICE!

You can treat a lionfish sting on your own, but it's best to get checked for any complications.

YOUR ADVENTURE CONTINUES
AUSTRALIA

The pain is worse than when the snake bit you! You clean the wound with soap and water, then go to the emergency room. There, the medical professionals check for broken-off lionfish spines under the skin, disinfect the wound, and apply heat in order to break down the venom and speed up your recovery. After observing you to make sure you don't have an allergic reaction to the venom or other complications, you're cleared to go.

The next morning the pain is mostly gone. You decide to give the beach a miss and go instead on a trip to the bush to see some wildlife. You're 10 yards (3 m) from a magnificent red kangaroo when it comes toward you and rears up to its full height. It's about to attack! What do you do?

CHOOSE YOUR SURVIVAL

OPTION 1

Run.

(JUMP TO PAGE 78.)

OPTION 2

Sidle away slowly and try to get behind cover.

(JUMP TO PAGE 74.)

OPTION 3

Fight the kangaroo.

(JUMP TO PAGE 76.)

LIONFISH
STING

OPTION 2

Perform first aid,
then apply heat to
the wound.

OKAY, BUT NOT THE BEST CHOICE

Most people don't die from lionfish stings.

If you're stung by a lionfish, it's important to make sure there are no broken-off pieces of the venomous spines in the wound. If there are, gently pull them out. Clean the wound with soap and water, then with an antiseptic pad or alcohol. If you're bleeding, put pressure on the wound to stop it. Next, soak the wound in the hottest water you can stand for at least half an hour. This makes the lionfish venom break down faster.

The first aid might be all you need, but there could be complications. There might still be pieces of the spines in your skin that you can't see. The wound could become infected. You could have a deadly allergy to the venom. It's even possible that the venom could paralyze your arms or legs. You can't treat any of these things by yourself.

ARE YOU SURE YOU'RE NOT ALLERGIC?

JUMP BACK TO PAGE 51 & CHOOSE A BETTER OPTION

A lionfish sting is painful but usually not fatal. Unless you're allergic to the venom. Are you sure you're not allergic to the venom?

NOT THE BEST CHOICE

Ice will keep the venom in your system longer.

A lionfish sting doesn't hurt much at first, but soon becomes very, very painful. After cleaning the wound you might be tempted to ice it to treat the pain and make the swelling go down. But the cold will actually slow down the breakdown of the venom in your system, lengthening the time it takes the pain to go away. The venom breaks down faster with heat.

Lionfish look fearsome and spectacular, with their stripes, long fins, and as many as 18 needle-sharp spines on their backs. The spines are covered with venom. The fish grow to be about 8 inches long. They're popular with people who keep saltwater aquariums. They're also now an invasive pest on the Atlantic coast of the United States and in the Caribbean. The invasion may have been started by aquarium owners releasing unwanted lionfish into the wild. The problem? Aside from their venomous stings, lionfish eat any animal that fits in their mouths, and they have no natural predators. They're gobbling up the native fish.

Some people think the solution to the invasive lionfish problem is to eat them. Minus the spines, of course.

ICE WILL ONLY MAKE THINGS WORSE

JUMP BACK TO **PAGE 51** & CHOOSE A BETTER OPTION

GOOD CHOICE!

Floating on your back is
the best way out.

YOUR ADVENTURE CONTINUES
AUSTRALIA

Quicksand is more than half water. Lying backward, it's easy for you to float on the surface. With the weight off your legs you're able to wiggle them little by little to create some space around them. That lets the water seep in to re-liquefy the packed sand. After a lot of wiggling you're finally able to extract both legs. Still on your back, you pull yourself to firmer ground. You're saved!

The next day you decide you've had enough of the ocean. You take a trip to the rural area called the bush to look at some of the famous Australian wildlife. You're 10 yards (3 m) from a magnificent red kangaroo when it comes toward you and rears up to its full height. It's about to attack! What do you do?

CHOOSE YOUR SURVIVAL

OPTION 1
Run.

(JUMP TO PAGE 72.)

OPTION 2
Move sideways slowly and try to get behind cover.

(JUMP TO PAGE 74.)

OPTION 3
Fight the kangaroo.

(JUMP TO PAGE 76.)

NOT THE BEST CHOICE

Surely you've figured that out by now.

Run? Really? Did that work with the snow leopard or the rhinoceros? Red kangaroos can hop along at 35 miles per hour (56 kph), jump higher than your head, and cover 25 feet (7.6 m) in a single bound. They can support themselves on their tails while aiming powerful kicks at your stomach with their clawed hind feet. Their forepaws have sharp, slashing claws, and they use their teeth as weapons as well.

Red kangaroos are the largest marsupials in the world. They live in the plains and deserts of central Australia. They travel in groups called mobs, some with hundreds of kangaroos. Females give birth to one tiny, blind baby at a time. The newborn kangaroo climbs into its mother's pouch and grows there for two months without coming out.

RED KANGAROO

(Macropus rufus)

LENGTH: UP TO 5 FT. (1.5 M)

WEIGHT: UP TO 200 LB. (90 KG)

TAIL: AS LONG AS 44 IN. (1.1 M)

TOP SPEED: 35 MPH (56 KPH)

LIKE ALL THE ANIMALS YOU'VE MET SO FAR, A RED KANGAROO IS FASTER THAN YOU ARE

JUMP BACK TO PAGE 71 & CHOOSE A BETTER OPTION

KANGAROO
ENCOUNTER

OPTION 2

Move sideways
slowly and try to
get behind cover.

GOOD CHOICE!

Putting a barrier between
yourself and the kangaroo
is the best way to defuse
the situation.

YOUR ADVENTURE CONTINUES

LOS ANGELES

An attacking kangaroo will kick at your abdomen with its hind legs, so you turn sideways to protect the front of your body just in case. Keeping your eyes on the animal, you edge slowly away until there's a thick clump of bushes between yourself and it. After a tense minute the kangaroo decides you're not a threat and goes back to its mob.

You head back to the city, unscathed but more than ready to head home. Your flight leaves the next day. You have a three-hour stopover in Los Angeles. You're waiting for your connecting flight, going through your trip pictures on your phone and looking back on all the narrow escapes you've had, when the building starts shaking. It's an earthquake! What do you do?

CHOOSE YOUR SURVIVAL

OPTION 1

Run! Get outside as quickly as possible.

(JUMP TO PAGE 80.)

OPTION 2

Stand in a doorway. It's the strongest part of the building.

(JUMP TO PAGE 82.)

OPTION 3

Take cover under a desk or table and wait for the shaking to stop.

(JUMP TO PAGE 84.)

NOT THE BEST CHOICE

The kangaroo is stronger than you are.

Fight a kangaroo? Are you kidding? You wouldn't stand a chance. It has you outweighed and out-powered. A male red kangaroo can weigh 200 pounds (90 kg) and stand taller than 6 feet (1.8 m) on its hind legs. Those legs have powerful muscles that can carry the kangaroo on a 25-foot (7.6-m) leap or fire a slashing kick at your abdomen. If attacked, don't try to fight a kangaroo! Protect yourself instead.

Male kangaroos can be aggressive if they think their territory or mates are being threatened. Females will attack to defend their young, called joeys.

YOU CAN'T FIGHT A KANGAROO AND WIN. BETTER TO RETREAT SO THE KANGAROO DOESN'T ATTACK YOU

YOU HAVE ENTERED A WILDLIFE SANCTUARY

DO NOT FEED
THE
KANGAROOS!!

- **FEEDING HUMAN FOODS IS DETRIMENTAL TO KANGAROOS HEALTH**
- **KANGAROOS ARE UNDOMESTICATED ANIMALS THAT CAN CAUSE INJURY.**

DON'T FEED THE KANGAROOS!

You might think kangaroos are cute (you'd be right!) but they're wild animals, and you definitely shouldn't feed them. Visitors to a popular kangaroo-viewing area in Australia had been feeding the animals. Trying to get carrots and other snacks, some kangaroos went after tourists with claws and kicks. Now the site has signs warning people not to feed them.

JUMP BACK TO **PAGE 71** & CHOOSE A BETTER OPTION

NOT THE BEST CHOICE

You may be fast, but a red kangaroo is faster.

With their powerful hind legs, kangaroos travel fastest by hopping. A red kangaroo can cover as much as 25 feet (7.6 m) of ground with each hop. That gives it a top speed of 35 mph (56 kph), way faster than you can run. When it catches up with you, the kangaroo can slash you with its razor-tipped front claws. It can also sit back on its tail to kick you in the stomach with both hind legs at once. You wouldn't stand a chance.

RED KANGAROO

(Macropus rufus)

LENGTH: UP TO 5 FT. (1.5 M)

WEIGHT: UP TO 200 LB. (90 KG)

TAIL: AS LONG AS 44 IN. (1.1 M)

TOP SPEED: 35 MPH (56 KPH)

YOU CAN'T OUTRUN A RED KANGAROO

SUPER FIGHTERS

It's best not to annoy a red kangaroo. With large males standing as tall as 5 feet (1.5 m) and weighing as much as 200 lb. (90 kg), they're the world's biggest marsupials. Male red kangaroos fight each other for mates. The fights are for dominance, in other words to determine who's the boss, but the fighters can still end up with broken bones or internal injuries. Females will also fight to defend their joeys, or young kangaroos.

JUMP BACK TO PAGE 65 & CHOOSE A BETTER OPTION

NOT THE BEST CHOICE

Running to the exit isn't safe.

When an earthquake hits, you might panic and think you need to run outside right away. What if the building collapses with you inside it? But running to the exit can be more dangerous than staying put. First, running on a floor that's heaving under your feet isn't easy. There's a chance it could shake hard enough to knock you down. Second, by traveling through different parts of the building you're actually increasing the chance of being in a place where a falling or flying object could hit you. Finally, if you do get to the exit, the space right next to the outside wall of a building is where you're most likely to get hit by a falling piece of architecture, like a window or decorative part of the building.

When the shaking starts, if you're inside stay inside and protect yourself. If you're outside, stay outside and move away from buildings, trees, and power lines.

Wait till the shaking stops. That's the time to get out quickly if the building has been damaged.

IT'S BETTER TO STAY PUT AND PROTECT YOURSELF

JUMP BACK TO **PAGE 75** & CHOOSE A BETTER OPTION

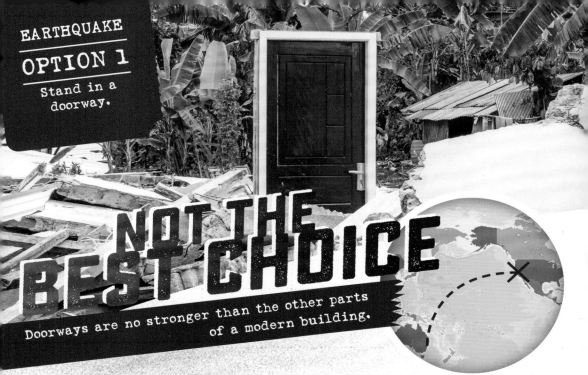

NOT THE BEST CHOICE

Doorways are no stronger than the other parts of a modern building.

While the door frame may have been one of the stronger parts in the wall of an old-fashioned building made of bricks or adobe, modern buildings are built out of reinforced materials to keep them standing in an earthquake. The biggest danger in an earthquake comes from falling or flying objects, and standing in an open door frame won't protect you from those.

In the United States, states and cities where earthquakes are more likely to happen have building codes that require extra reinforcement. That makes buildings, bridges, and highways stronger in case of a big shake. If you live in one of those places you may also have heard of something called "seismic retrofitting." That means adding extra earthquake reinforcement to older buildings and other structures.

Even if you're in an old, unreinforced building, a strong piece of furniture will protect you from falling objects better than a doorway.

DOORWAYS DON'T GIVE YOU EXTRA PROTECTION

JUMP BACK TO **PAGE 75** & CHOOSE A BETTER OPTION

EARTHQUAKE

OPTION 3

Take cover under a
desk or table and
wait for the
shaking to stop.

GOOD CHOICE!

When an earthquake hits,
drop, cover, and hold on.

YOUR ADVENTURE CONTINUES
LOS ANGELES

You crawl under a nearby table and hold onto one of the
legs. Once the shaking stops, you get out and see if anyone
needs help. The people around you are okay, but the shops
on the airport concourse are a mess of objects that have
fallen off the counters and shelves.

No flights will be leaving the airport for a while. In
fact, yours has been canceled. You decide to go sightseeing
in the city. You visit the observation deck of a new
skyscraper for amazing views all around. On the way down,
the elevator suddenly lurches to a stop, drops two feet,
then stops again. You're afraid the elevator will plunge
down the shaft! What do you do?

CHOOSE YOUR
SURVIVAL

OPTION 1

Press the alarm button and wait for help.

(JUMP TO PAGE 86.)

OPTION 2

Pry open the elevator doors and climb out.

(JUMP TO PAGE 88.)

OPTION 3

Climb out of the roof hatch on top of the elevator.

(JUMP TO PAGE 90.)

ELEVATOR
PLUNGE

OPTION 1

Press the alarm
button and wait
for help.

GOOD CHOICE!

If you're stuck in an
elevator, the best thing to
do is wait for help.

YOUR ADVENTURE CONTINUES
HEADED HOME

You press the alarm button and talk to an emergency dispatcher over the intercom. After a 20-minute wait, an emergency crew opens the doors from the outside. The elevator is suspended three feet above the building floor, but the crew helps you to climb out safely. When you turn and look back, you see a dark gap in the doorway below the bottom of the elevator. It leads to a 40-story drop!

The next day you're finally on a plane on the last leg of your long and hazardous adventure. You arrive safely at the airport and catch the bus home. The weather is looking a little grim. When you get out at your bus stop, you feel a few drops of rain. You decide to get home more quickly by taking a short cut through the park. There's a flash, followed almost instantly by a crash of thunder, and the rain starts pouring down. It's a thunderstorm, and you can't get home and safely indoors without crossing an open soccer field!

CHOOSE YOUR SURVIVAL

OPTION 1

Take shelter in the trees at the edge of the soccer field.

(JUMP TO PAGE 92.)

OPTION 2

Go inside the restroom building.

(JUMP TO PAGE 94.)

OPTION 3

Run across the field on tiptoe to minimize your contact with the ground.

(JUMP TO PAGE 96.)

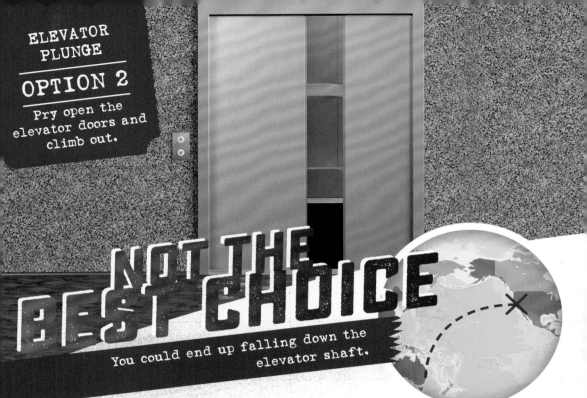

ELEVATOR
PLUNGE

OPTION 2

Pry open the
elevator doors and
climb out.

NOT THE BEST CHOICE

You could end up falling down the
elevator shaft.

You know from the floor indicator that the elevator has
stopped somewhere between the 40th and 41st floors. If
you could pry the doors open, you might discover that the
elevator is just below the 21st floor, with the actual floor
up at your eye level or higher. Even if you could climb
up, the gap between the building floor and the top of the
elevator door might be too small for you to fit through.
Worse, the elevator might have stopped a few feet above
the 40th floor, leaving a big gap between the floor of the
elevator and the floor of the building. If you tried to climb
out and slipped through the gap, you'd find yourself hanging
by your fingertips above 40 stories of empty elevator shaft!

PUTTING ON THE BRAKES

Without elevators, there would be no skyscrapers. And without safety brakes there would be no elevators. The first elevators were raised and lowered by ropes or chains. In 1852, an inventor named Elisha Otis came up with an automatic brake that would prevent an elevator from plunging to the ground if the rope or chain broke. That made elevators safe enough for people to ride in.

CLIMBING OUT OF A STUCK ELEVATOR ON YOUR OWN ISN'T SAFE

JUMP BACK TO **PAGE 85** & CHOOSE A BETTER OPTION

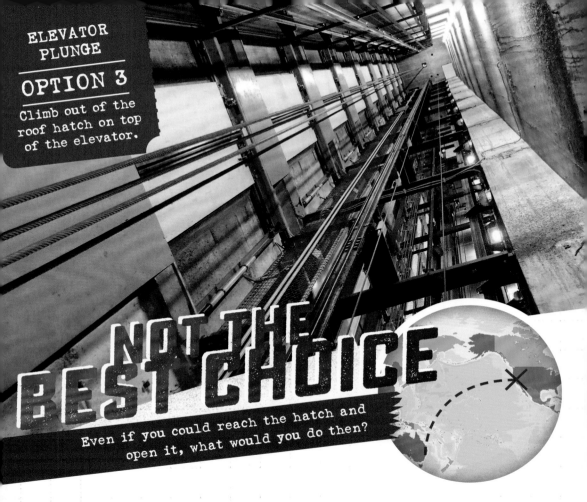

OPTION 3

Climb out of the roof hatch on top of the elevator.

NOT THE BEST CHOICE

Even if you could reach the hatch and open it, what would you do then?

For starters, how would you reach the hatch? It's in the ceiling above you, and there's nothing in the elevator you could stand on. For another thing, it's probably locked. The roof hatch is made for maintenance or emergency workers to get in from the outside, not for passengers to open from the inside. Finally, even if you could reach it, open it, and climb out, what would you do then? You'd be on top of the elevator, with 40 stories of open shaft above you.

SAFETY FIRST. AND SECOND, AND THIRD.

Elevators have multiple safety systems. The motor brake stops the cab at each floor. This brake only opens if there's power applied to it, so if there's a power failure, the elevator stops automatically. There are two or more ropes. Each of them could hold the elevator up by itself. Finally, even if all the ropes should break, safety brakes underneath the cab will clamp onto the rails and keep the elevator from falling.

THE HATCH ISN'T MADE FOR ESCAPING

JUMP BACK TO PAGE 85 & CHOOSE A BETTER OPTION

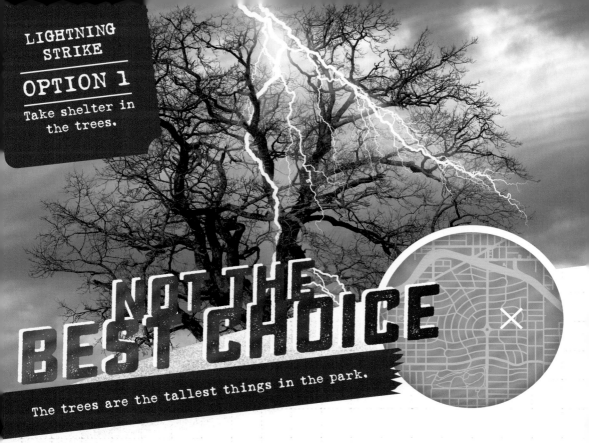

NOT THE BEST CHOICE

The trees are the tallest things in the park.

Come on, everybody knows it's a bad idea to stand under a tree during a thunderstorm! Okay, really, it depends. It's probably safer to stand by the trees than in the middle of the empty soccer field. And if you're somewhere with a lot of trees, like a forest, you're better off there than in a clearing. But the only clump of trees in an otherwise open park isn't the best bet for lightning safety.

If you stand by a tree in a thunderstorm, you're in danger of being hit by a side flash, also known as a side splash. A side flash happens when lightning strikes a tree, and some of the current jumps from the trunk to a nearby person. It usually happens when the victim is standing within a few feet of the trunk. Of course, that's where you'd stand if you wanted to get out of the rain.

Lightning current can also travel through the ground around the tree. This ground current is especially dangerous because it can cover a large area. It's the cause of the most lightning-related injuries and deaths.

TREES ARE GOOD SHELTER FROM THE RAIN. FROM LIGHTNING, NOT SO MUCH

JUMP BACK TO **PAGE 87** & CHOOSE A BETTER OPTION

LIGHTNING
STRIKE

OPTION 2

Go inside the
restroom building.

GOOD CHOICE!

An enclosed building is
the safest place to be in a
thunderstorm.

YOUR ADVENTURE CONTINUES
AFTER THE STORM

It's not the nicest place to wait out the storm, but the park's restrooms are in a real building with a foundation, walls, and a roof. Your chances of being injured there are much less than if you were outside. Open structures like picnic shelters or bus stops might seem safe, but they're not.

Inside the restroom you avoid touching the sink fixtures and pipes. It's still possible for lighting current to travel through the ground into the pipes. You wait for the storm to pass, then continue on your way. There's a rainbow, and you stop to sit on a bench by a pond to admire it. You drop your backpack on the ground against a tree trunk. You hear angry buzzing and feel a sharp sting. You've disturbed a nest of yellow jackets! The wasps come swarming out of their nest. What do you do?

CHOOSE YOUR SURVIVAL

OPTION 1

Jump in the pond and stay underwater till the yellow jackets leave.

(JUMP TO PAGE 98.)

OPTION 2

Slap the wasps that land on you before they get a chance to sting.

(JUMP TO PAGE 100.)

OPTION 3

Run away!

(JUMP TO PAGE 102.)

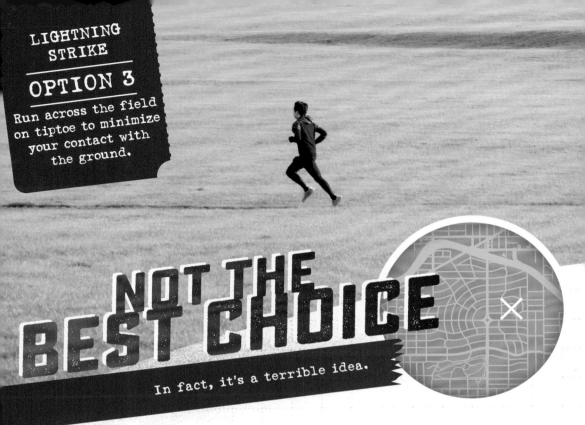

LIGHTNING
STRIKE

OPTION 3

Run across the field
on tiptoe to minimize
your contact with
the ground.

NOT THE BEST CHOICE

In fact, it's a terrible idea.

If you run across the soccer field, you'll be the tallest thing in the middle of a big, open space. That makes you a prime target for a lightning strike. It doesn't matter how much of you is touching the ground. It doesn't even matter if you're touching the ground at all. You've seen lightning travel through the air between clouds and the ground. It wouldn't have a problem going through you to get there.

A lightning bolt is a bit like a giant version of the static spark that snaps between your finger and a doorknob after you shuffle across a carpet. Believe it or not, in most cloud-to-ground lightning strikes, the visible flash travels up from the ground to the cloud. It's lightning fast, about 200,000,000 mph (320,000,000 kph)!

RUNNING ACROSS A FIELD DURING A THUNDERSTORM IS A SPECTACULARLY BAD IDEA

WHAT ARE THE CHANCES?

Your chance of being struck by lightning in a particular year is one in a million. What that really means is that one person out of every million in the United States will be struck by lightning. Your real chances depend on where you live and how often you go outside in a storm. If you run across a soccer field in the middle of a thunderstorm, your chances are much, much higher.

JUMP BACK TO **PAGE 87**
& CHOOSE A BETTER OPTION

OPTION 1

Jump in the pond
and stay underwater
until the yellow
jackets leave.

NOT THE BEST CHOICE

You'll have to come up to breathe, and the wasps will be waiting for you.

Sure, the yellow jackets won't be able to sting you while you're underwater (provided the pond is deep enough!) But even if you're a super breath-holder, you'll only be able to stay there for a few minutes before coming up for air. That's not long enough for the wasps to lose interest and go away. They'll be hovering over the pond, and the moment your head breaks the surface, they'll make a beeline for you. Worse, now you're stuck in a pond, where it's even harder to get away.

"Yellow jacket" is the common name for several different wasp species. Some build nests underground, while others nest in trees, rotting wood, or even inside the walls of houses. They're famous for their bad tempers, attacking aggressively if their nests are threatened.

THE YELLOW JACKETS CAN WAIT LONGER THAN YOU CAN HOLD YOUR BREATH

JUMP BACK TO **PAGE 95** & CHOOSE A BETTER OPTION

YELLOW JACKET
ATTACK

OPTION 2

Slap the wasps that
land on you before
they get a chance
to sting.

Pretty much
everyone hates yellow
jackets, but they do help
control other insect
pests by hunting them.
The problem is that often
the yellow jackets become
pests themselves.

NOT THE BEST CHOICE

If you thought the lionfish sting was
painful, wait till you feel the venom
of a dozen yellow jacket stings.

You only have two hands, and there's a whole swarm of
yellow jackets chasing you! Even if you manage to kill
a few of them, the rest will still be after you, with
possibly very serious consequences. Unlike honeybees, which
sacrifice their lives to sting once, each yellow jacket can
sting many times. A swarm of angry yellow jackets can sting
you with enough venom to put you in the hospital, even if
you're not allergic.

CHEMICAL COMMUNICATION

Yellow jackets communicate with chemicals called pheromones (FAIR-uh-mones). If you disturb their nest, the wasps emit alarm pheromones that alert others that the colony is under attack. The same thing happens if you squash a yellow jacket, which is another reason slapping them isn't a good idea. Worse, every time one of the yellow jackets stings you, she leaves some of the alarm pheromone on you. It's a chemical message that says, "Here's the culprit! Quick, sting right here!"

SLAPPING YELLOW JACKETS IS FOOLISH AND DOWNRIGHT DANGEROUS

JUMP BACK TO PAGE 95
& CHOOSE A BETTER OPTION

GOOD CHOICE!

At long last, running is
the answer.

YOUR ADVENTURE CONTINUES

ALMOST HOME

Running is finally the best choice. You grab your pack and take off with the yellow jackets in hot pursuit. The only way to escape a swarm of these wasps is to run and keep on running as fast as you can until the yellow jackets decide you're no longer a threat and return to their nest. You get a couple of painful stings, but you escape. Luckily you're not allergic to wasp stings.

Finally, your house is in sight! You can't wait to tell your family about your adventures, all the amazing things you've seen, and all the narrow escapes you've had. You bound up the front steps with a smile on your face, but the yellow jacket stings must have made you a little dizzy. You lose your balance and fall backwards down the stairs! What do you do?

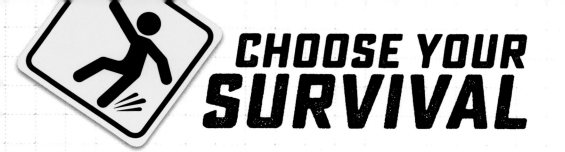

CHOOSE YOUR SURVIVAL

OPTION 1

Keep your body as stiff as possible so it acts like a spring.

(JUMP TO PAGE 104.)

OPTION 2

Twist and put out your arms so you can catch yourself on your hands.

(JUMP TO PAGE 106.)

OPTION 3

Tuck, pivot, and roll.

(JUMP TO PAGE 108.)

FALL DOWN
STAIRS

OPTION 1

Keep your body as
stiff as possible
so it acts like a
spring.

NOT THE BEST CHOICE

Tensing up is more likely to get you injured.

It's a natural reaction to tense up when you feel yourself falling. But if you're stiff and tense when you hit the ground, you're actually more likely to get injured. If your body and limbs are bent, the flexibility can help to absorb the shock of impact. The most important thing to protect in a fall is your head. If it hits the ground with force, you could get a concussion—a serious brain injury that happens when you hit your head or body hard enough to make your brain bounce or twist inside your skull.

PROTECT YOUR HEAD

If you're falling backward, tuck your chin to your chest, so your head doesn't hit the ground if you land on your back. If you're falling forward, turn to the side, so you don't land on your face.

PROFESSIONAL FALLERS

Movie stunt performers, paratroopers, and martial arts experts all know how to handle falls. Their advice? Protect your head, relax, stay loose, and distribute the impact to your body. Now all you have to do is keep that in mind as you're tipping backwards off the front porch.

DON'T TENSE UP

JUMP BACK TO PAGE 103 & CHOOSE A BETTER OPTION

FALL DOWN STAIRS

OPTION 2

Twist and put out your arms so you can catch yourself on your hands.

NOT THE BEST CHOICE

That's a good way to break something.

Doctors and emergency room professionals have a word they use to describe a set of injuries they see a lot. It's FOOSH, which stands for "Falls On OutStretched Hands." When falling, a natural reflex is to try to catch yourself with one or both hands. But with your arm stretched out and rigid, you're likely to sprain or break your wrist, hand, or elbow. It's better to keep your arms and legs close to your body, relaxed and bent to absorb the impact of the fall.

Stunt professionals, martial artists, and other people who fall all the time as a part of their jobs have another piece of advice: land on the meat, not on the bone. That means falling on the fleshier, more muscly parts of your body like your outer thigh or rear end. You may end up with bruises, but it will help you avoid a broken elbow, knee, or shoulder bone.

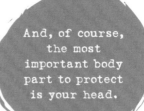

And, of course, the most important body part to protect is your head.

AVOID A FOOSH!

JUMP BACK TO PAGE 103 & CHOOSE A BETTER OPTION

GOOD CHOICE!

The best way to absorb the
shock of a fall is to roll
with it.

YOUR ADVENTURE CONTINUES
ALMOST HOME

As you start to fall backwards, you pivot to your side to
avoid landing on your back, tuck your chin to your chest
to protect your head, and curl with your arms and legs
bent and close to your body. The meaty part of your thigh
hits first (ouch!), then your body rolls with the fall
(oof!), and you keep on rolling (ow!).

Instead of all the force of the fall being concentrated
in one place like your hand or elbow, it gets distributed
over as much of your body as possible. Winded, you sit on
the ground for a minute to catch your breath. You can feel

the bruises, and the yellow jacket stings still hurt like nobody's business, but you didn't hit your head, and you haven't broken anything.

You pick yourself up, dust off your clothes, and walk back up the stairs to the front door. This time you hold onto the railing.

YOU'RE ALMOST THERE!

TURN THE PAGE

YOUR ADVENTURE ENDS

HOME AT LAST

You're finally home! Your family listens with amazement as you tell them about the adventures you had, the parts of the world you saw, the amazingly bad luck you ran into as you faced one brush with disaster after another, and the amazing skill and good sense that got you through all of it in one piece.

You think about it as you relax later on the couch. It really was pretty amazing! You faced fierce and venomous animals, natural and human-made perils, accidents, fires, and a fall down the front steps. (You didn't mention that last one to your family, and you really hope nobody saw it.) Not everyone gets a vacation like that!

You turn on the television to see what's new. The show is interrupted by a long tone and a notice from the Emergency Broadcast System. There's a tornado warning in effect...

Brimming with creative inspiration, how-to projects, and useful information to enrich your everyday life, Quarto Knows is a favorite destination for those pursuing their interests and passions. Visit our site and dig deeper with our books into your area of interest: Quarto Creates, Quarto Cooks, Quarto Homes, Quarto Lives, Quarto Drives, Quarto Explores, Quarto Gifts, or Quarto Kids.

Published in 2020 by becker&mayer! kids, an imprint of The Quarto Group, 11120 NE 33rd Place, Suite 201, Bellevue, WA 98004 USA.

www.QuartoKnows.com

becker&mayer! kids titles are also available at discount for retail, wholesale, promotional, and bulk purchase. For details, contact the Special Sales Manager by email at specialsales@quarto.com or by mail at The Quarto Group, Attn: Special Sales Manager, 100 Cummings Center Suite 265D, Beverly, MA 01915 USA.

21 22 23 24 25   6 5 4 3 2

ISBN: 978-0-7603-6880-0

Library of Congress Cataloging-in-Publication Data available upon request.

Author: Paul Beck
Design: Scott Richardson
Editorial: Betsy Henry Pringle
Production: Tom Miller

Printed, manufactured, and assembled in Malaysia, 5/21.

Image credits: All stock photographs and design elements © Shutterstock

#336491